how
to be
a human

to write
is to break your soul
into pieces
and scatter the fragments
on the pages.

love is like
water
it can keep you afloat
or
it can drown you

the first time i met him
he told me about
how he had terrible anxiety
and was quite embarrassed by it
and i envied him
for being so open and honest
in a way i could never be
even though i wanted to
yet it felt inappropriate for me
to tell someone who gets
nervous in public
that i see demons
and wonder if
there are cameras hidden
behind his clear blue eyes.

- *psychosis*

how can a world with so many beautiful things
possibly be so ugly
how can the earth
and soil
be so treacherous
when it is filled with wildflowers
wrapped in sky
how can something so lovely
be so devastating
it is because
of the human beings
who make this world cruel
and harden its heart

your touch
makes me flinch
it feels so much like his

i tell you about the loss
the grief
and a sorrow fills the room
heavy and heartbroken
so i recite to you
quieter times
gentler times
softer times
this
this, this, this
is how i explain to you
that even though i have lived through
so much bad
i have still managed
to find the good

place your hands
on my heart
or my hips
i don’t care which

i will never
ramble to you
about the kinds of teacups
my therapist keeps
on her desk.

i will never
tell you
the kinds of artwork
my psychiatrist hangs
on his wall.

but i swear to tell you
my hopes
and my fears
and my dreams
should that be what you'd like to know.

weeds
pushing through
cracked pavement
are the most beautiful of all
to think life exists
where it shouldn't at all

your bones creak
as i sleep
and it keeps me awake
as the wind howls outside.

i met a murderer once
he stuck his fingers
down my throat
his hands
tasted of salt
from the tears
of lives he took
and of sugar
from the lives he touched.

everything i ever lost
has been returned to me
but i can't help feeling that
i am missing something
very important

i smashed every camera
and speared the watching eyes.
dark corners float
in my vision so i
destroy until i forget
and i pick up the shards
when the sun rises.
even though they are gone
it doesn't help
because their blood
is on my hands.

all my friends left me
because i killed them.

- a loss of empathy

You trace the furrows over my eyebrows, the frown lines from years without hard work, years of muted softness and shattered bones. A paradox made from a paradox. You romanticize the death, the yellow paint and the way it kills so poetically; you find beauty in what is not and never will be – sick, sick, sick; you and I are Sick. You are the little black bird that follows me around. You are the razor blade glinting from our twin necks, our shared wrists. You are the means and the end, and you justify yourself.

I am crying now, dewdrops that sting like alcohol, whiskey that reeks of your crooked smile.

I—L-O-V-E-D—Y-O-U.

I am snapping the stalks off sunflowers in my hands, despairing that humans must destroy themselves before finding salvation. If only we had never reached this point.

You feed me salt and tell me it is sugar; you laugh like a crow when I recoil at the taste. And so I begin to thank you when you give me what I have deserved all along, thanking you with my palms pressed together that, Good Lord, today is a day you chose not to hurt me. So then They come for us, all of them, with their broken hands and broken hearts and we are a drunken team all of a sudden, thrown together and sanded down like rocks in the ocean. And I cannot take it anymore, the loss of contact, the loss of sharp edges and blood.

At least, yes, at last – at least you are dead now.

i never write about you
because i am afraid
to split myself open
and stitch myself back together.

a way to pass the time has always been
to be a collector of secrets
to hold their knowledge
between your fingers
so when they try to cut you down
with their knives
you can throw it all back in their faces.

i think when you left
you took part of me with you

- it's probably why i feel so empty

i saw your face
for the first time in months
it was only a reflection but
it has haunted me
since.

i am
low on patience
low on empathy
low on love
i am
not afraid
of losing you anymore

i know i am supposed to be strong
but the truth is
i would do anything
just to have you by my side again

- what did i do wrong?

listen to me
the world
is
crueler
kinder
scarier
sweeter
deadlier
safer
than you could ever believe

no matter how hard i slammed my hands down
my knuckles never bled enough
no matter how hard i screamed
it was never quite loud enough
the broken words left my lips over and over
i am tired of being treated like shit
for those i trip over myself for

– i used to love you, you know

you just don't understand
i never loved you
not at all
you were just
a placeholder
a convenience
a comfort
and i feel
no guilt
no remorse
but my god
it did shock me to hear
how empty your voice sounded
on that warm may afternoon.

you have touched
my hands
but never
my soul

I have a black dog who follows me around all the time, who bays when I am angry and howls when I am in mourning. I have a black dog who has spent every day of his wretched life begging for scraps from my plate, who takes and takes and takes but never gives, only watches from a distance, thumping his feathered tail against the floor - gently, gently—ever so gently. I have a black dog who watches me with intelligent eyes, always thoughtful, always cautious. He raises his nose to sniff the air. He can sense my fear, I know he can. I have a black dog who knows all my thoughts and dreams and hopes and fears; I have a black dog who knows how to destroy me.

But I will never let him.

Please don't be offended. You must understand. My trembling hands. My shaking voice. I will always wonder. If you work for the government. If you hate me. If the images that flash behind your eyelids as you sleep are ones of knives entering my skin. If you do this. If you do that. If you are with Them.

Please don't be offended.

Please don't be offended.

You must understand.

i have had my heart broken
and i lived
you will too
i promise

i poured
my heart and soul
into everything i did
i poured
and poured
and poured
and now
i'm left empty.

it's a complete disconnect from reality it's voices over
and over and it's dead and decapitated and mutilated
animal corpses that follow you everywhere with
razors stuck in their necks it's social isolation it's not
showering for days it's curling up on the ground
because you are terrified of everything and it's
believing the love of your life is trying to kill you
being crazy is not cute and being crazy does not mean
you are a quirky twelve-year-old being crazy is

scary.

i know it ends here
i know our book
has been finished
closed
forgotten
but ours
will always be
the greatest love story
this world has ever known.

other girls
are smart
and sweet
and sensitive
other girls
are bright
and brilliant
and beautiful
there's nothing wrong
with being like
other girls.

– *"you're not like other girls"*

he spat at me with his eyes closed,
bitterness evident in everything he did.

The first great love of my life wandered in when I was three. He stayed for thirteen years, patient and kind and sometimes demanding, lulling me to sleep in tides of security, flowing like water and wind and all the pure things of the earth. Freedom. Self-rule. Older, I grew older, and the older I got the less I had these things, the more my love became about straight lines and numbers on sheets of permanent records stained with coffee in some mysterious back room where everyone smokes cigarettes and waits for phone calls. Even as the sovereignty I so admired about my love waned, I still thought he would stay forever. Bullshit. It was bullshit! I wrote seven thousand and eighty-nine papers on absolute and unfiltered bullshit! I devoted my meager hopes and miserable dreams to this beautiful concept of Autonomy.

Autonomy! Ah, yes! Stain a tea bag with cat piss and call it my love. *Ninety.* Pour my heart and soul into broken fingers and bloody paint tubes. *Seventy-five.* Autonomy, you see, she is lovely in theory but has no hopes of reality here, here in this goddamn place where to be special is to be wonderful, to be ordinary is to be no one at all; lovely in *theory,* ma'am, but poor in execution - have I lost you yet? Shall I simplify? Ah:

I am falling out of love. There are flowers growing everywhere: in my ribs, in my lungs, in my heart; they are spilling out of my mouth too, so I pick them all up and give them to Autonomy, begging her to please bring my love back, *please i won't ever ask for anything again if you could just bring him back, make him come back to me, i miss him so very much, please* - she tells me to quiet, to hush, that it is too late. There is nothing she can do now. The flowers I pulled from my conscience were not enough.

(In the past, I suppose they would suffice, but not in these days, not in this place.)

it seems i have
misunderstood
miscalculated
misjudged
what it means to be a human being.

the collision
of our souls
was the sweetest thing
i have ever witnessed

when she cries
she looks like
a heroine
but
when i cry
i am a shot
of pure heroin.

if you bloom
and they try to cut you down
do not poison them
do not cut them
with your thorns
just grow
grow to the sky
and don't stop

Sometimes I lie in bed. In complete darkness. And wrap a hand around my throat so I can feel my pulse. Gently. Quietly. I wonder what it would feel like. To take that away from someone else. What does it feel like? To look at your hands and know they have killed. Tell me.

I see pieces of you everywhere. Sometimes I see cats lazing in their yards. I think of you. Of how you wrapped your hands around the neck of your cat. Until you heard the snap. And watched the light leave its eyes. How you laughed.

We don't know where that man hid the body of the person he killed. I don't know. You don't know, either. But the person you killed. You must know where the body is.

This isn't Schrödinger's paradox. The cat is dead. After all, you killed him. So. Please. Get. Away. From. Me. This is all wrong.

You didn't even know my name.

- a letter to Evan

you are the focal point
the center of gravity
the coins at the bottom of the fountain
that people made their wishes on.

you are the sky
the sunlight
dappling through the trees
that warms my bones.

i see us as the sun
shining
radiant
and burning
to a violent
and fiery death

at the end of the day,
a stage is just a stage.
it is the actors
that give it life.
i only sing in my dreams.
we twist crowns
of daisies and ivy
and i don't have time
to think about any of the bad things.
instead of my beautiful someone
i see someone else's
beautiful someone
sunning in the wildflowers
our hands weave ropes out of.
but this too is only
another well-crafted lie
on the stage of sleep.

i
am not
in control.

She inspires me in ways I could never write. To keep going. *Don't end it there.* A faint smile on her lips, cheering me from the sidelines. A gentle glow. The Summer encouraging the Spring.

I have learned that we curl into ourselves before we die, burning bright before burning out. Our lives were lent to us, someday we will loan them back. Am I speaking of stars or humans? I do not know; they are the same to me. But not to her. She sees grace in all she touches. I am furious, so furious, that the world has taught her she is not beautiful, for there is a softness in her that is more striking than any supernova.

She inspires me in ways I could never write. To try again. *Just one more time.* A familiar look in her eyes, rooting for me behind the scenes. A blinding brilliance. The Summer chasing the Spring.

There is a warmth in her, a light, a star that never dies. A graciously broken girl by an ungraciously broken world, a ray of light looking for an exit through the cracks. There is a gentleness in her, the brave soul who does not fear thinking the world a wonderful place. A greatness in her courage, her soft-spoken courage.

She inspires me in ways I could never write. I am an artist, not suited in the game of words. But she. She is a miracle born from ink and pen.

Thank you for everything.

- *Katherine*

i never needed you to save me
i needed saving
from you.

you underestimated me
walked on me
talked down to me
for years
and once i finally succeed
you wish to act as if
you have been here
all along

except for the shattered bottles
it was like you'd never been here
at all.

- the case of the disappearing alcoholic

what i learned in one year:

1. they don't love you anymore.
2. she never loved you.
3. he loves you. a lot.
4. you love him. a lot.
5. remain kind in difficult situations.

my eyes were so full of sadness that it was
pouring out of them in a torrent,
an unbridled rush, but your eyes
were only a drizzle or a mist
a few light drops, nothing
like my storm yet all the
donations, volunteers
well-wishes, prayers
went to your cloud
and not a soul
even noticed
the hurricane
drowning
me.

you are
a force to be reckoned with
and your face
is permanently
etched into my memories

there are ghosts here
that lurk in the shadows
tucked away in dark corners
all the people
who received from the universe
a little more than they gave.

- selfish

the person who came after me
was a replacement
but it didn't make me feel any better because
i was a replacement too

you should compare
the difference between
smoke shop miseries
and real-life joys.

Do you think there's some alternate universe where we're still together, musing about some alternate universe where we're not together?

i swear
i will see stars in your eyes
until the day we die.

There are three sides of a triangle:
the Father, the Son, the Holy Spirit;
three forms of destruction
in life: birth, love, and death.
Don't cry, my love.
Destruction is not the end; resurrection is not
the beginning. I thought for sure
you knew this, thought for sure
you would take my side.
Thought for sure I was
more to you than
the girl who held herself so far above
the rest of us. Love smiles gently down
upon us and bathes us in golden light, tinted
like the sky before a storm.
Something is amiss.

I can't tell the difference between life and death.
It all looks the same.

they were the most
beautiful broken couple i had ever seen
like the sun and moon
always separating at the end of the day.

i saw them glance across the room
and their eyes met for a very long heartbeat
when i told the class i was
doing a project on first loves.

although i did not know either of them well
i saw months and months flash before my eyes
the sun and the moon remembering each other
one last time.

- the most beautiful broken couple

how many people
do you think you've already seen
for the last time?

- a thought to ponder

her poetry
is made of magic and sugar
and none of it rhymes

I hope they stare at you like you are the first sunrise they have ever seen in their life. I hope they see fragments of you scattered in every beautiful thing on this earth, and I hope they tell you when you cross their mind. I hope they will think about all the times they swore they would never be happy again and I hope they will look over at you falling asleep during class and realize they were wrong. I hope they are gentle with you, and take their time with you, and understand that life has already been hard enough. I hope they love you with the kind of love that is wild heartbeats and weak knees and parted lips. I hope they love you with the kind of love that is serenity and peace and the feeling of coming home. I hope they call you at 2 a.m. when they're falling apart, but also at 2 p.m. when they're on top of the world. Most of all, I hope they are thankful. I hope they thank God every day for you, and if they don't believe in God, I hope they remember to thank the universe every day for the miracle of loving you.

- i hope you love them

you shine
through your brokenness
bits of mirror
or shattered glass
reflecting
the moonlight.

i am
so many people
all at once
a kaleidoscope of
innocence
anger
treachery
love
kindness
cruelty
swirling together
and colliding

i only love him
when you're not looking

i have stardust
running in my veins
and the ocean
roaring in my heart
you cannot tell me
i am one of you

if you leave
then you must
stay gone.

our love is
the purest and rarest
form of love.
our love is
flashing white teeth
and falling leaves.
our love is
milky sunrises
and fluttering eyelashes.
our love
is the greatest love
ever to exist
in the history
of the universe.

i regret what i did to you
and i'm sorry
i regret leaving
the hurt
the sorrow
the pain
the emptiness
the loss
i regret it all
and the same words
pour from my lips over and over

- i'm sorry.

creator
and destroyer
he is both

you can live forever
that's the joy
of being young and in love

- but you die as soon as it's over

he looks at me
like i am the sun
and what i mean by that is
like any person with sense
he doesn't look at me
at all

- anna karenina

i wish young boys knew
that it's okay
to wear flowers in your hair
and to let gentleness
flow from your soul
as much as it's okay
to be tough and strong
if that's what you want.

- lessons we should teach our sons.

to have your successes
diminished
simply because of your race
is quite possibly
one of the most frustrating experiences.

- it's because you're asian, isn't it?

there is so much suffering in the world
and it feels like
it's impossible to conquer
but if you can
lessen the pain of anyone
even just a fraction of a degree
i promise
that means all the world
to someone

whenever i was sad it was always you who
so graciously comforted me. when i said
i wish i could be like her
you said
i like you the way you are and when i
thought my art was a mess you told me
i think it looks lovely
it didn't matter if i was happy or sad
or hurt or heartbroken or having a
perfect day or a terrible day
you always sat with me and told me that
things were good
and i miss that very deeply.
i remember the day
i cried to you
why doesn't he love me and you said
i'm sorry i'm sorry i'm so sorry
which was exactly what i needed to hear
rather than mouthfuls of
excuses and false comforts so
thank you for everything
and i will
probably still hear your voice for years
but it's a small price to pay for
all the wonderful times we had together.

goodbye.

maybe things
can change
maybe it doesn't
have to end like this
maybe we'll
never know.

We can never go back to the way things used to be because the people we were when we met are very, very different from the people we are today.

your pain
is *nothing*
compared
to my
superior
suffering.

- delusions of grandeur

if you love yourself
you'll never
die alone.

the person you love
is supposed to make you happy.

i'd rather have
my heart
feel content with my work
than change it
to fit the demands
of those around me.

I run through the city streets at 3 a.m., decapitating those stray cats who linger around concrete corners.

I'm up at 6 a.m., covering my lips in sugar and honey, sweet-talking strangers.

I'm far, far away by 10 a.m., rushing through this world in an ultraviolet haze.

My mind is racing 90 miles an hour by 3 p.m., a chorus of light and color spilling through my veins.

I always return, though, at 5 p.m. on the dot.

Why? Why? Why do I always return, only to leave again before the sun rises?

Because ____________________.

love is:

a. a little bit luck
b. a little bit coincidence
c. a little bit fate
d. a complete miracle
e. all of the above

i write poetry he says
i wrote something for you
the words, the phrases
something about it is all off
it's the sickly sweet aroma
of too much extravagance
that makes his musings
about me
impossible
to swallow

did you see it?
look, there
flashing quickly
in the periphery
the man
who comes out
of the mirror
to haunt
these young bones

i lost
a constellation
of stars
that i loved
to the
endlessness
of space.

i lived through
heartbreak
trauma
grief
loss
and
sixteen
years
later
here i am, still
surviving
still
making stardust
of it.

i am tired of trying to convince myself
that i should keep my mouth shut
for the convenience of others
if i have to speak
then i shall
simple as that

you were
the love of my life
the loss of my life
the last of my life.

i don't have an agenda against alcohol
i have an agenda against those
who care more about alcohol
than their
children
families
friends
loves.

- it's a damn shame.

i don't think
i've ever hated anyone
as much as i hate you

- a letter to myself

it's okay
if they're gone
those thoughts you had
of *yes, he's the one*

the bright side to the trauma she says
is that you have something to write about
i stare at her as if she's lost her mind
as if
all the months
of blood
horror
tears
were simply
something to write about

the first time i saw you
i glimpsed a flash of your hair
in the library aisles
as you selected your favorite book

and there was a spark
of recognition
the first time i ever looked
in your eyes

and you smiled at me
when i asked who you were
and said,
i'm your lifelong companion.

- *first impressions*

you were the first person
in my entire life
i had completely to myself

i have to let that go

i have to let go

Scuffling bags. Strangers coughing. I crouch in my seat, my spine pressed against the cushioned back, waiting, waiting, waiting.

He was supposed to be here
thirty minutes ago.

There is magic here, in the waiting, the clamoring, the rush of people from all walks of life filling the air with the rhythmic tapping of their steps.

He was supposed to be here
forty minutes ago.

If I blur my eyes, that stranger over there – yes, him, with the brown hair – if I blur them, it almost looks like you.

He was supposed to be here
fifty minutes ago.

My eyes are still blurred; is that you, walking across from the terminal? It must be, yes, it *must*–

He isn't
coming.

What're you feeling?

Nothing. Nothing at all.

- *the delayed flight*

being broken is not always beautiful
sometimes it means
picking up the pieces
and gluing things back together

but just ‘cause you’re broken
doesn’t mean you’re not exquisite

you are the sum
of your experiences.

so make them count.

i built myself from
all the pieces
you threw away

it was a stab in the heart
how quickly you decided
forever wasn't what you wanted anymore.

choose me
abuse me
use me
lose me.

- i still can't give you my soul.

you underestimate me but
make no mistake
i have sat across from the devil
and stared him straight in the eyes.

- december

i wondered
how i would ever be able to fix you
if i cut my fingers
on your broken edges
everytime i went near.

so what's the big deal
with this girl you keep
talking about?

she's got
the prettiest eyes
that glisten when
she talks about what she loves

her laugh oh god
it sounds like a wild goose
but no one minds 'cause
it's her truly enjoying herself

i think she's so so pretty
but she never believes me

i just think of you when i’m on my own
because playing make-believe
is more comforting
than sitting alone.

i wrote every sweet thing you ever said about me
down on fresh white paper
in blood-red ink
struck a match
and set that motherfucker on fire
in my kitchen sink
laughed as the flames swirled
death to you and me

- *backstabber*

i don't believe
in necessary evils
i think the world
to be sweet as sugar
and i believe
softness will follow you
wherever you go
if you only
let it.

i try not to write about you because
i know if i start
i'll never stop
and as a person of my word
i know *never stopping* means
something goes on forever
which clearly was a concept
you promised
but didn't understand.

I always thought of you as my city, as my hometown, as a place where I memorized every traffic light and intersection and storefront like the back of my hand. Coming to you was like collapsing down at home at the end of a long day, but now. Now I have returned and I recognize nothing – it's like a dam has been released, flooding every memorable landmark with water, drowning it in the depths of distortion. The outside is still the same. Your laugh. The houses. Your eyes. The neighborhoods. But suddenly everything is totally wrong. The florist is selling automobiles, the bakery is holding a funeral. Your words sound hollow and empty. Nothing is how it should be.

My hometown has been destroyed, and you are gone.

this house
is so cold
without you
in it.

why am i the target
whenever you shoot arrows
why must they be towards me

why am i the dartboard
when you aim
why must it be for my heart

why am i the vase
when you feel angry
why must it be me you shatter

i'll
always
remember
what
you
did
to
me.

it was the most dysfunctional
group of people
given the hardest task
a crowd of
young cat-killers
murderers
liars
thieves
given the terrible, terrible job
of staying alive

- the psychiatric ward

i'm sorry i said to you
i have someone i love
with a grin you said *he doesn't have to know*
and that was when i knew
i had to get away

you weren't special
it wasn't you i needed
it was anyone

it is important to try to love yourself
understand that
but also know
the phrase *no one will love you*
unless you love yourself
is a lie
love will come
love will always find you
no matter what

hold me
like i am something delicate
hold me
like i am glass
hold me
like i am an atom bomb

- breakable

there will be other stars
but he was my sky.

a collision of two suns
can create a star
and now i know
exactly how you were born

i say i want to die
what i really mean is
i want to start living

They will promise you forever. They will sit next to you and see the stars in your eyes and hear the sea pounding through your veins. They will hear the thunder in your voice, realize what a wild storm you are. They will see all this, and they will make the promise anyway, unaware they are incapable of keeping it.

Then they will leave.

The promise will ring in your ears as you pick up your shattered pieces at 3 a.m., and you will spend every dawn through dusk wondering what you did wrong. Because they promised you forever, didn't they?

They will apologize. They will say they weren't *enough* to keep the promise – weren't old enough, weren't ready enough, weren't aware enough – whatever the case may be, *hold them accountable.* Hold them accountable for the cracks in your soul, the dark circles under your eyes.

And if they try to make excuses. Remind them. They promised forever. They promised always.

And breaking a promise, even if they didn't understand the enormity of it when they made it, well – if you break a promise, you had better hope your heart wasn't crossed.

isn’t it so odd
that the person you love
can become a stranger
as easily as a stranger
can become the person you love

- perspectives

you shatter a vase
you glue it back together

even though it shows
no signs of falling apart again
you are always checking
for more cracks

i want to be
the last person
you ever love.

if
he doesn't take the time
to listen to your favorite songs
you know – the ones that sound
like sugar and honey

if
he forgets about your habit
of making 11:11 wishes
you know – you always wish
to find the love of your life

if
he never notices
the tears in your eyes
you know – they have been coming
quite frequently now

if
he reaches for your hands
before your heart
you know – you should stop
wasting your time

why did you think
it was okay to
wander in when convenient
and break me
when it suited you

you were the one part of my future
i had figured out

now i’m stumbling through the dark
since you decided to turn the lights out

there are cracks covering his heart
that i am not meant to fix

- incompatible

the thing about
trying to grow in a toxic environment
is that the others
will stand on the sidelines, snarling
and if they see you succeed
they will belittle you
cut you down
destroy you
until you return to the shadows
and believe you belong there

- a school of the arts

you are enough
you have always been enough
you will always be enough
even if you break
even if you crumble
a moment of weakness does not
make you a person of weakness
even the sky
falls apart sometimes

you were born
to shatter chandeliers
and glass ceilings

sorry
i know there's something poetic about
comparing you to
a hurricane
a thunderstorm
a natural disaster
but to me you are much softer than that
a sunrise
a sunset
a sparkling star
something that fills the sky
with beauty
instead of destruction

happiness will find me
with or without you

we were sitting in a circle
in the psych ward
forced to
open up
and spill our hearts to each other

when it was my turn
i simply said
i want to go home

that's what
everyone else had said too

when it was his turn
he said it gruffly
and very insincerely
words pried
from his mouth by force
an involuntary confession

sarcasm dripped
from his chapped lips as he said
yeah, i want to go home, too

- *broken families*

i asked *how can you be so gentle*
if the rape destroyed you

she put her hands
on my shoulders and said

nothing is ever
destroyed beyond repair

mental illness
does not have to be beautiful
to be recognized

- society romanticizes what shouldn't be romanticized

i am angry
because i do not understand
that is your child
your blood
how could you fail
to protect them
from the abuse

fear should never be
at the heart of love

you didn't make me feel
more alive
you made me feel
less dead

teach me how to make coffee
your favorite way
and the flowers you like best
and the constellations
you find prettiest
teach me
how to dance in
the refrigerator light at night
teach me
to live with you
as a part of my life and
teach me
how to love
fiercely and fearlessly

to you
the alcohol is fun
to me
it is a tragedy

this book
was my
suicide
note.

i am tired of giving love
and receiving nothing in return
i pour my everything into everyone
my blood and tears
just for the happiness
of other people
only to have them turn around
and spit it back in my face
laced with venom

they did you wrong
they did you wrong
they did you wrong

now go forth
and set their world on fire

with
cat bones in my hands
and vengeance in my heart
god loosed me
upon the world
a harbinger
of death and destruction

i don't like sitting in
this cold and empty house
the floorboards creak
the windows rattle
the lights flicker
this is not the beautiful house
i once bought

i don't like sitting with
your cold and empty soul
you're nothing like
the bright and vibrant being
you used to be

i have so much soul to give
it runs through my veins
so much wonder and life
it overflows my bones
and drives me insane

one day you will die
so will i
and i thank god
for both of those things

philosophy is a privilege

it is a privilege to look at your hands
and wonder for the sake of knowledge
and not terror
if they are real or not

i curl up on the ground
because i believe i do not exist
the only thing running through my veins
is horror and confusion
i am not pondering the universe
i am scared to death

it is a privilege
to be stable enough
to wonder if you are real
without
the delusional side effects

- *philosophy*

i never want to be the girl
you write songs about because
all your songs break hearts

she thinks she's
nothing special
she once believed that the world
was a beautiful place but
it hurt her one too many times
still, even after the pain
she does not let herself spite others
she is still soft
and she hates it for she believes
people take advantage of her yet
i admire her for opening up her heart
to this earth, to its experiences
for remaining gentle
for remaining kind
she is strong
how can i tell her
she has the kind of soul
that makes me want to
create art

light me on fire
tear apart my world
add insult to injury by
walking away and returning
with a smile on your face

every time we fight
the earth spins off its axis
the stars shatter
and the universe
goes a little bit wrong

i don't want it to be like this anymore
i want to stop staring
at my hands
and the broken glass
wondering what i did wrong

i thought i could never hate you
even after all you put me through.

(i was wrong.)

you should let it go they say
but the problem with that
is that
i cannot forgive
as i never received an apology
i cannot forget
as every moment of the past
is permanently seared in my mind
i cannot just *let it pass*
i cannot let it happen
i cannot let go

- *scars*

there is yelling
there is screaming
there is the sound
of knives
entering flesh

there is crying
there is chattering
there is someone
telling me to
cut my own fingers off

but beyond that
beyond all of that
past the noise
there is you

there is only you
there is always you
snapping me back to reality
and saving me from the chaos
in my mind

i hate the phrase *you'll find someone*
so many people out there
never found their "someone"
what if i'm spending my life
wasting away, waiting for
a person who isn't out there

the hospital doctors
who knew me for a day
all described me as
impulsive
inconsiderate
lost
tormented
demanding
sick
but that doesn't bother me at all
because the people who i love
describe me as radiant

if you are looking for a sign
not to kill yourself
here is the sign

let me tell you that you are
the strongest, brightest
bravest human being i have ever witnessed

death and i walked
along the shore
skipping flat stones
and counting the clashes
of the waves along the beach
the thunder rolled in
and he asked me
why have you always wanted
to meet me so badly?

to which i replied
i thought it would be
more of a relief than this

the leaves fall
but they always grow back
civilizations rise and crumble
only to be replaced by newer ones
the world closes up on itself
and gives in to the frost of winter

one day you too shall break
but do not fear
you will come back
stronger than you were before

i wonder if you'll ever know
how many of these poems
were written about you.

- does that make you happy or sad?

how do you mourn a soul
that never died?

- december twenty-first, nineteen ninety-nine

i write because
my heart cries out
and i want someone to hear it

it was jarring because
where i expected light and life
there was only
a hollow reflection staring back at me.

- her eyes

all of us
every single one
was a human
even the cat-killer
even the girl who vomited after every meal
even the boy who stole from his mother
even the child who lived through abuse
even the man who murdered his friend
even me
every single one of us
was a human
is a human
deserves to be treated
as a human
and for a fee
on cloudy days only
if you catch us in the right mood
we can teach you
how
to be
a human.

thank you.

special acknowledgements

i. to my parents, for supporting me through this process as much as you've supported me for all sixteen years of my life.

ii. to coleman, my moon. thank you for lighting up my sky. thank you for believing in me when i couldn't believe in myself.

iii. to katherine – without you, this book never would have happened. stay soft and strong, love.

iv. to my dear and darling friends. you cheered me on through this project, read it in its first stages, and loved and praised it wholeheartedly. and thank you for taking such gentle care of me for all these years.

about the author

jennifer wilson is a high school student in metro-atlanta, georgia. her experiences with love, heartbreak, loss, psychosis, and life have inspired her to use writing as a platform to share her poetry. she resides at home with her parents, two dogs, and beloved evil cat.

Printed in Poland
by Amazon Fulfillment
Poland Sp. z o.o., Wrocław

53281824R00096